Birds

Written by
Stephen Rickard

This is a parrot.

A parrot is a kind of bird.

This is a penguin.

A penguin is a kind of bird.

This is a blackbird.

A blackbird is a kind of bird.

This is a robin.

A robin is a kind of bird.

This is a woodpecker.

A woodpecker is a kind of bird.